I LOVE YOU MORE THAN....

Written by
MADDIE FIGGIE

Illustrated by
NOELLE KOSTYACK

COPYRIGHT © 2014 MADDIE FIGGIE
ALL RIGHTS RESERVED.

ISBN: 1495382923
ISBN 13: 9781495382925
LIBRARY OF CONGRESS CONTROL NUMBER: 2014903388
CREATESPACE INDEPENDENT PUBLISHING PLATFORM, NORTH CHARLESTON, SC

Dedication

TO S. B. AND W. G. FOR LOVING ME MORE THAN ANYTHING.

~ Madeline

TO THE GREATEST FAMILY AND FRIENDS, WHOM I LOVE MORE THAN...ALL THE THINGS IN THIS BOOK.

~ Noelle

About the Author and Illustrator

AUTHOR MADELINE "MADDIE" FIGGIE RESIDES WITH HER FAMILY IN NOVELTY, OHIO, JUST OUTSIDE OF CLEVELAND. SHE ENJOYS READING, WRITING, GYMNASTICS, DANCING, AND PLAYING WITH HER PUPPIES, SKANDIE AND WEEGEE.

ILLUSTRATOR NOELLE KOSTYACK IS ELEVEN YEARS OLD. SHE STARTED DRAWING WHEN SHE WAS ABOUT THREE YEARS OLD AND HAS WANTED TO BE AN ARTIST EVER SINCE.

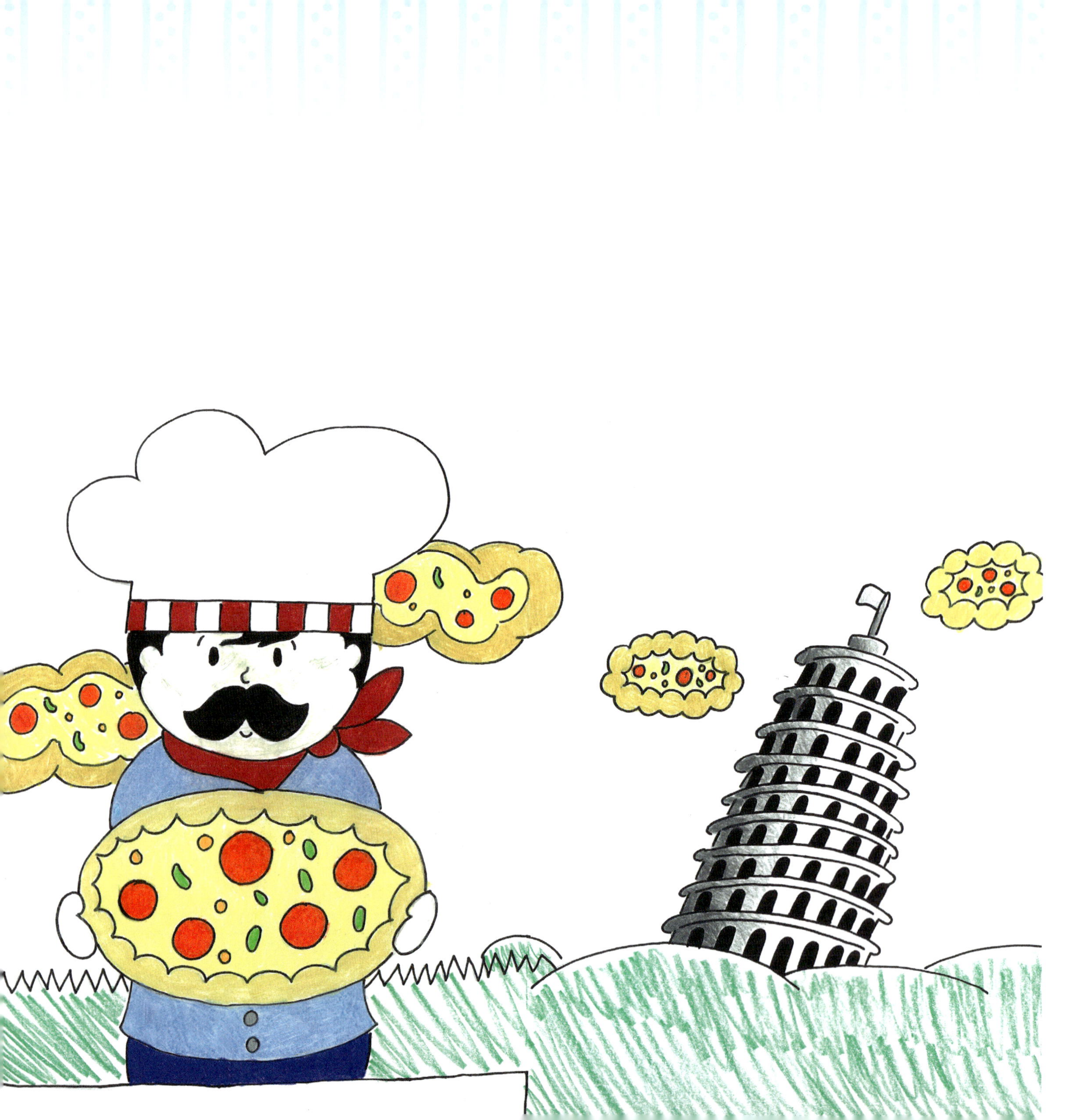

I love you more than...
all the pepperoni pizzas in Italy.

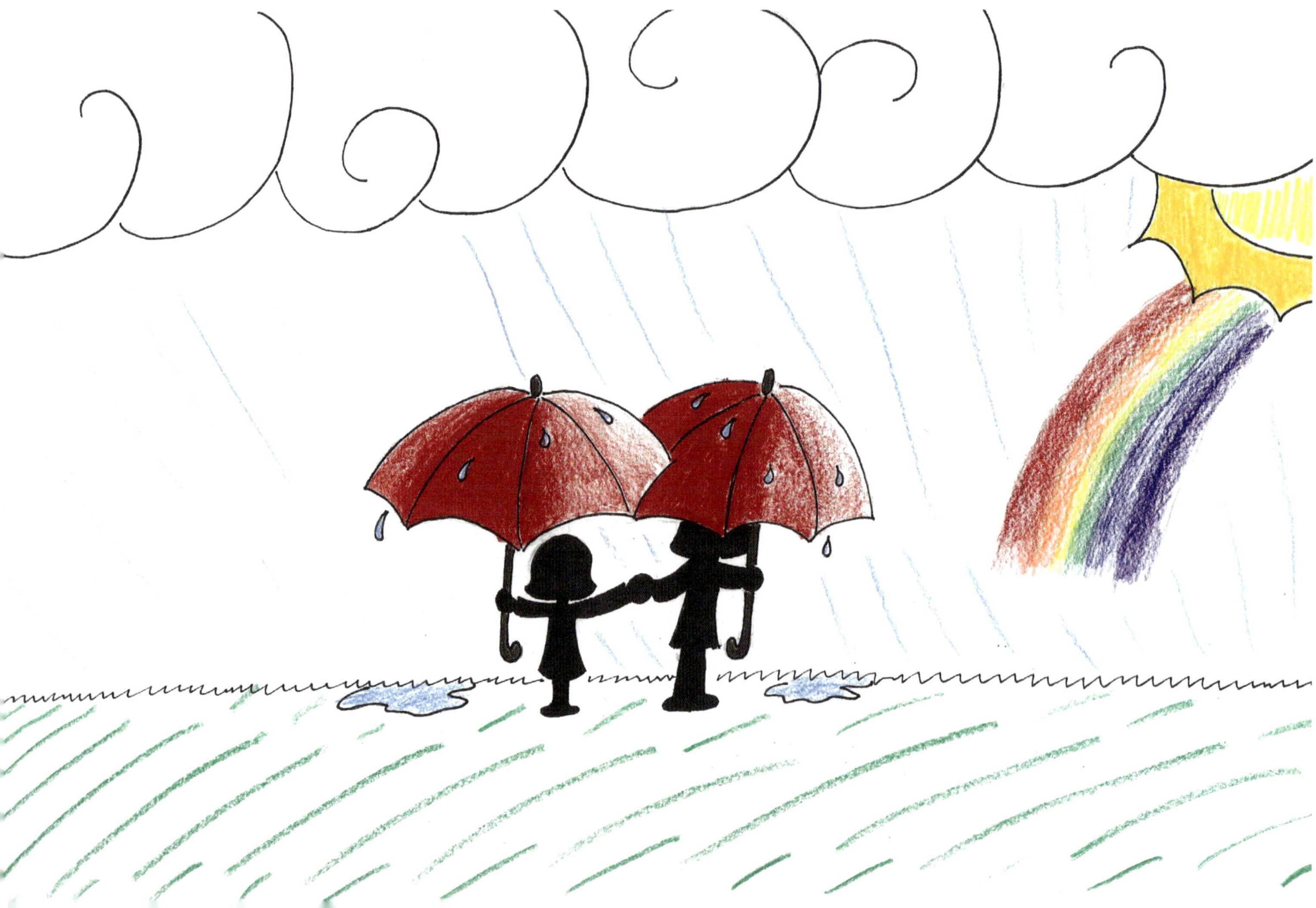

I love you more than...
all the raindrops
in a thunderstorm.

I love you more than...
all the shining lights
on the Eiffel Tower.

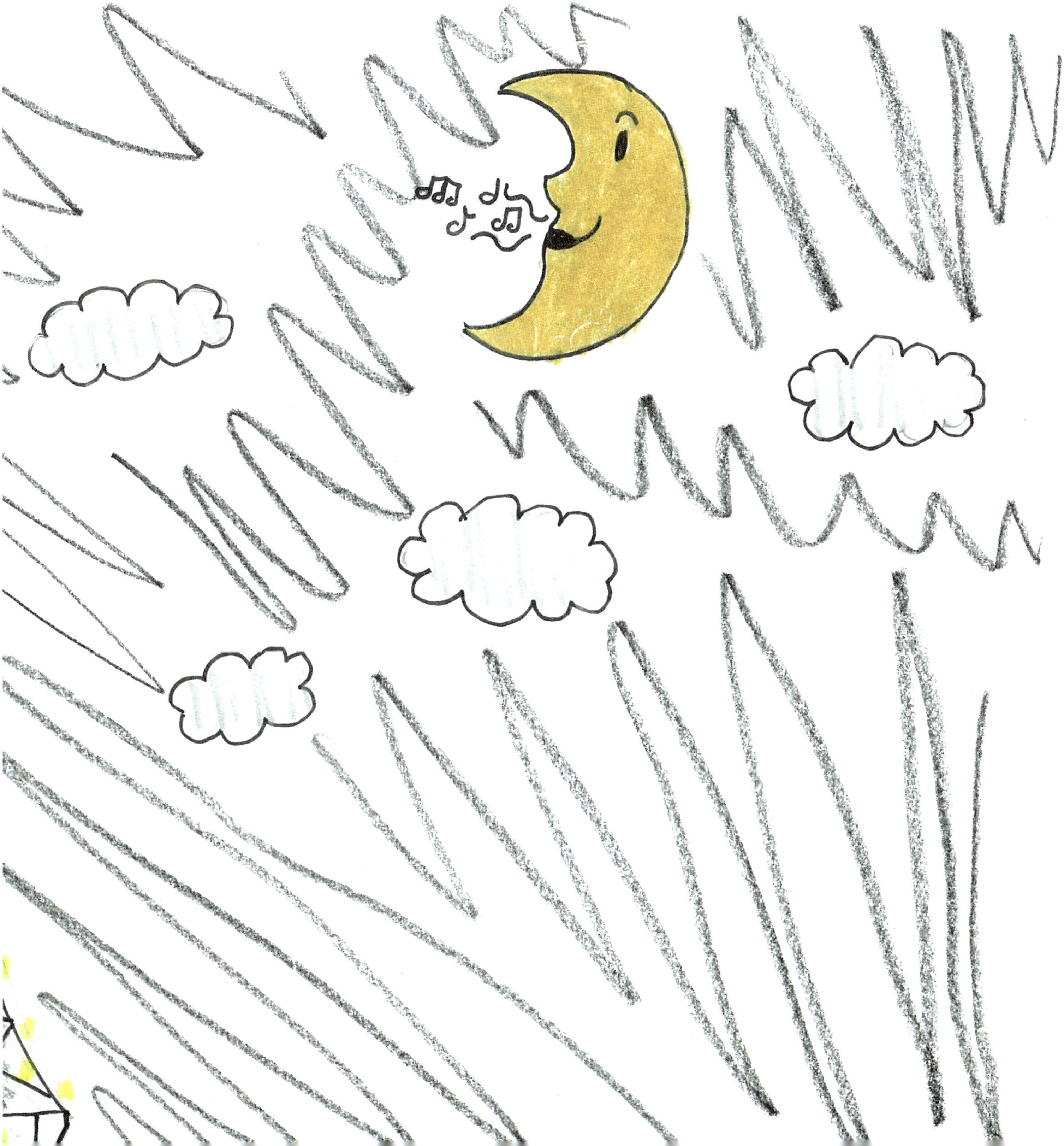

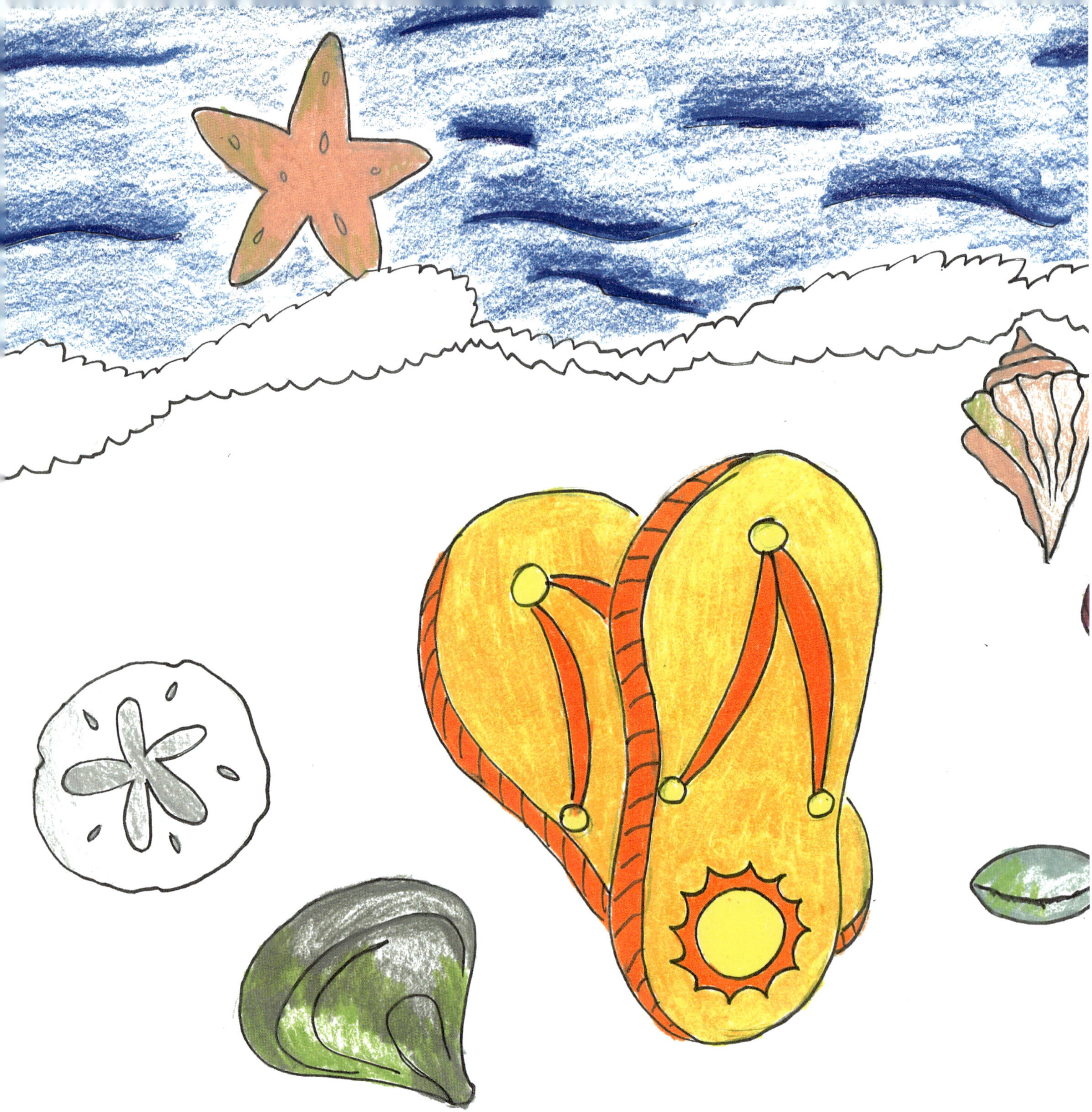

I love you more than...
all the seashells
on the beach.

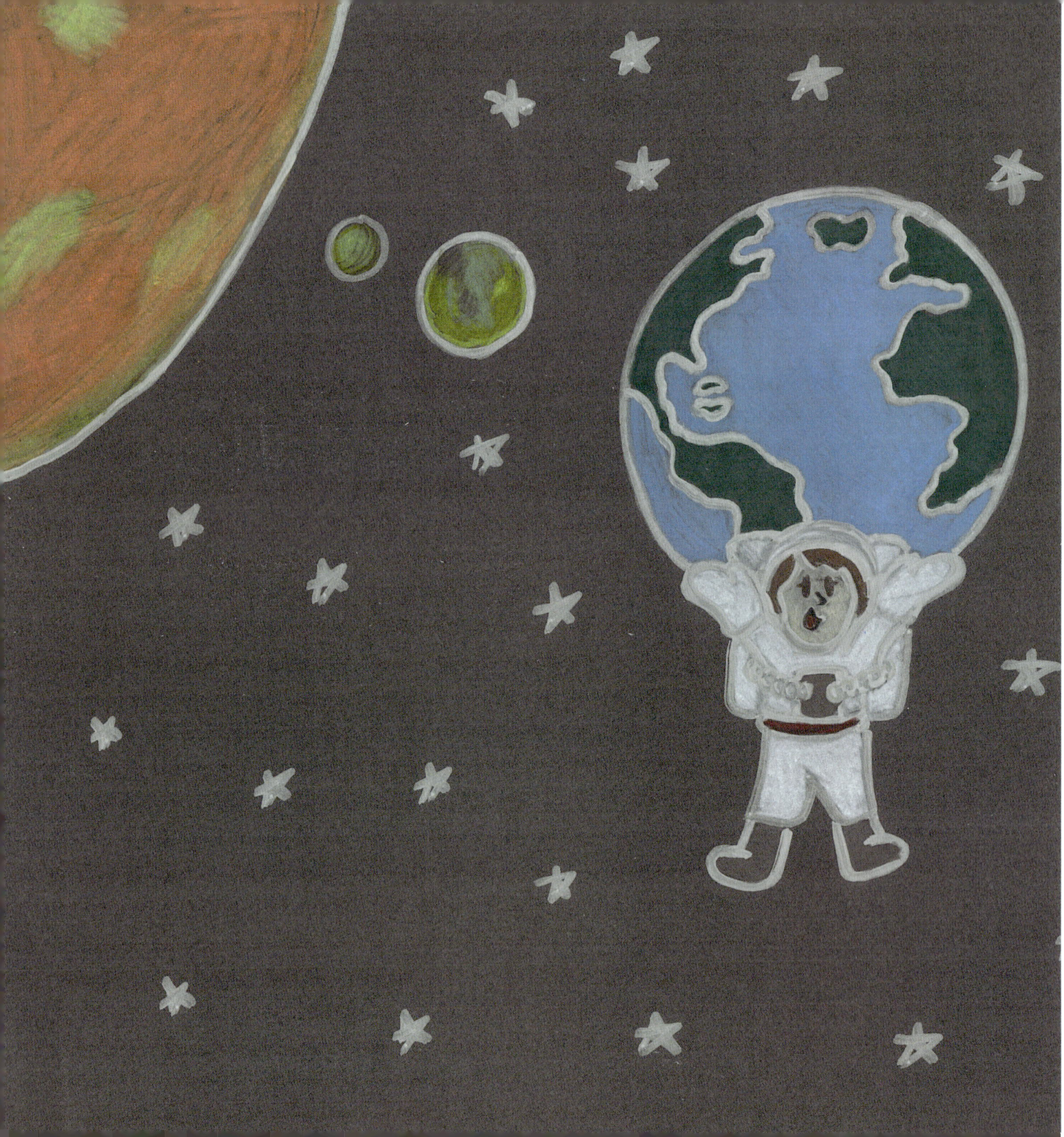

I love you more than...
all the stars in the
Milky Way.

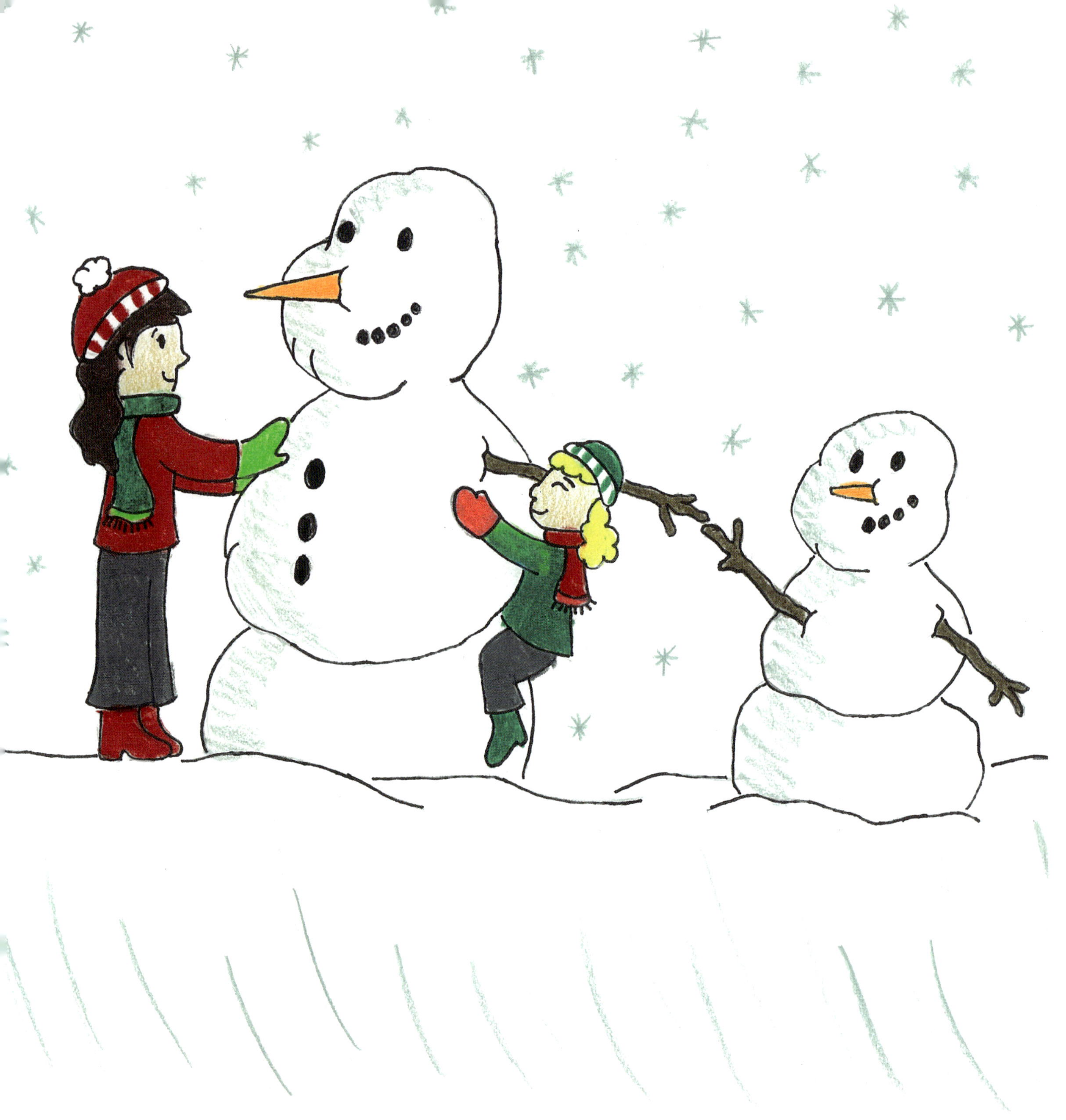

I love you more than...
all the snowflakes
in a snowman.

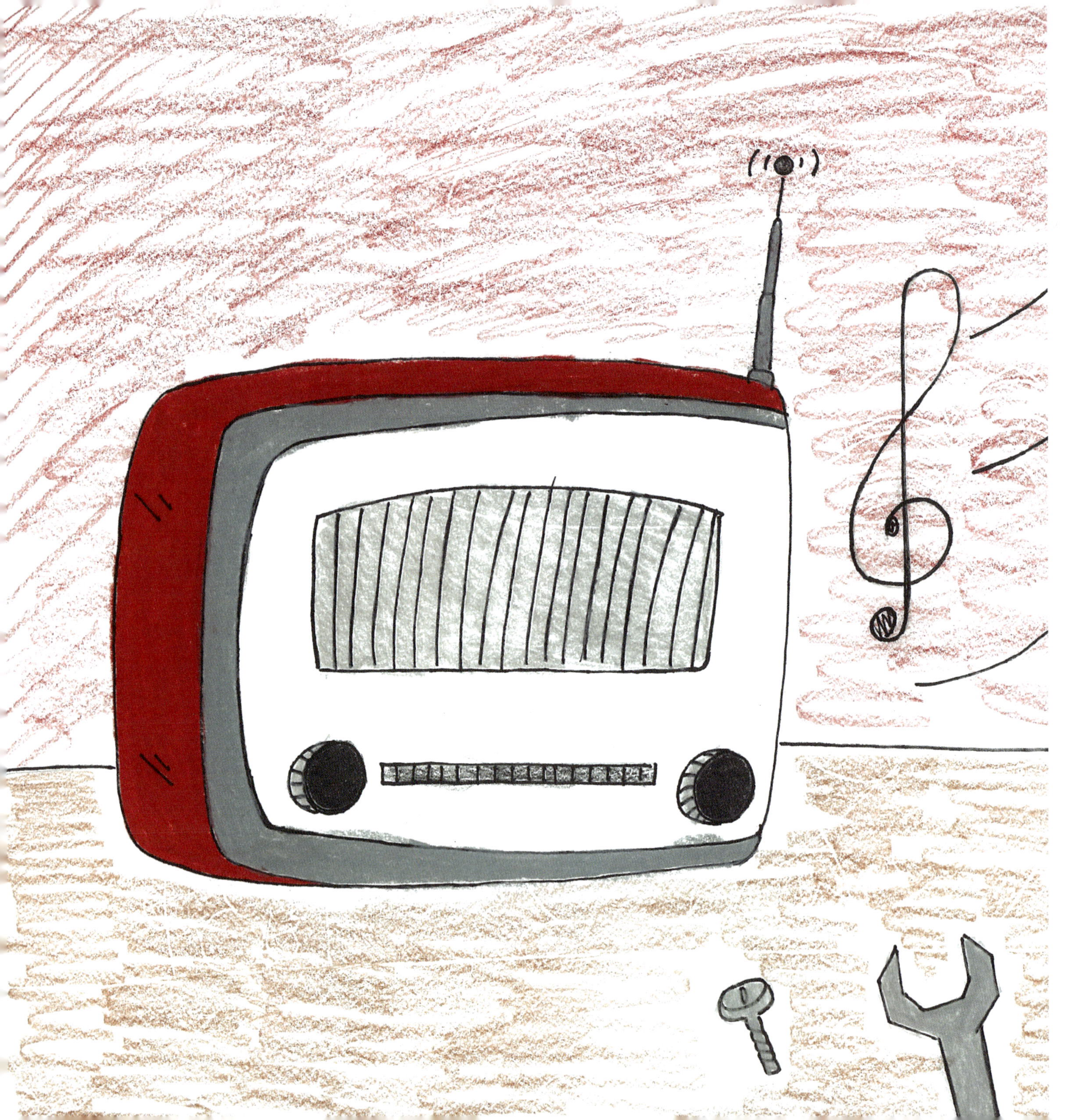

I love you more than...
all the songs on the radio.

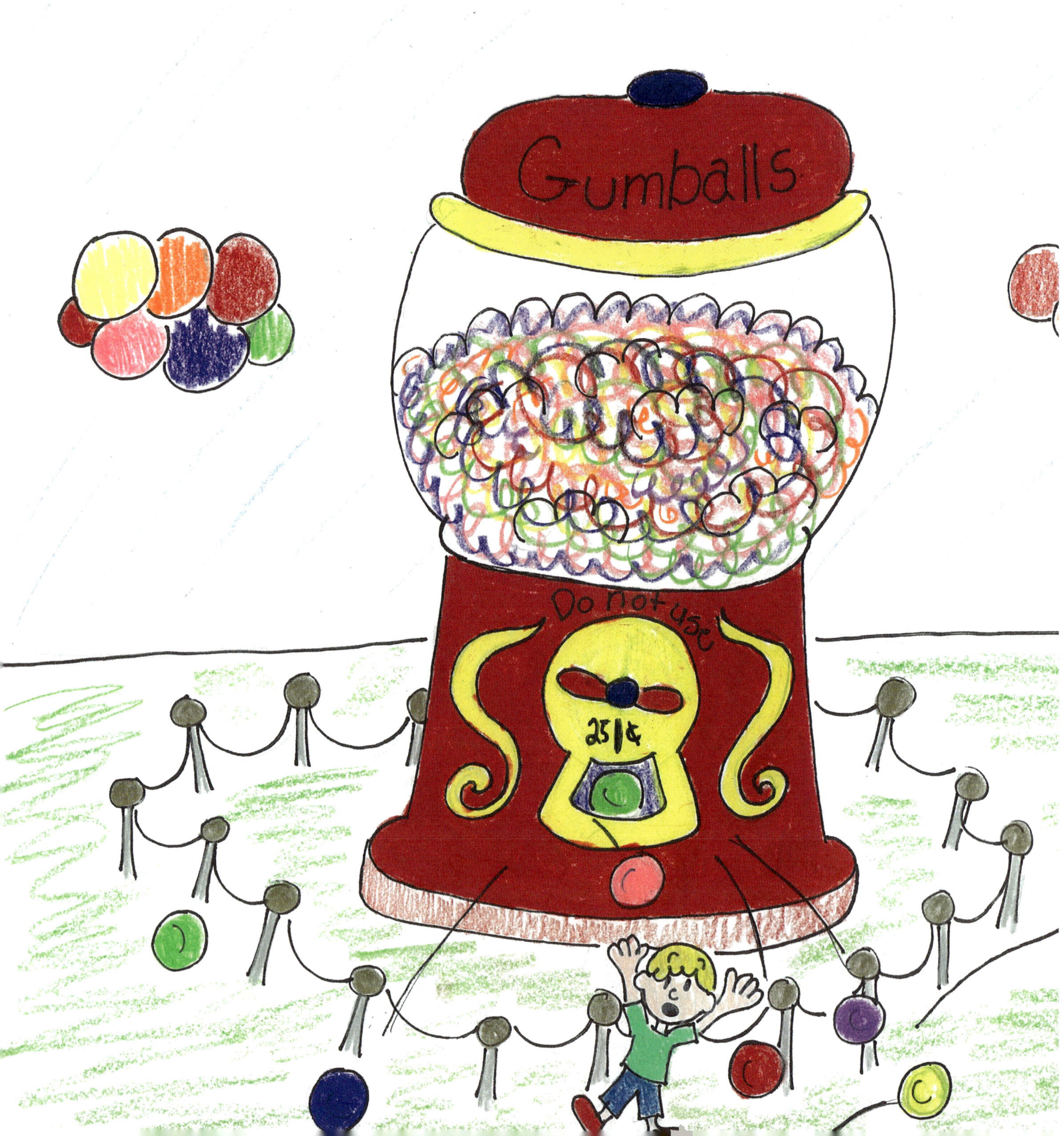
Gumballs
Do not use
25¢

I love you more than...
all the gum balls in the world's biggest gum-ball machine.

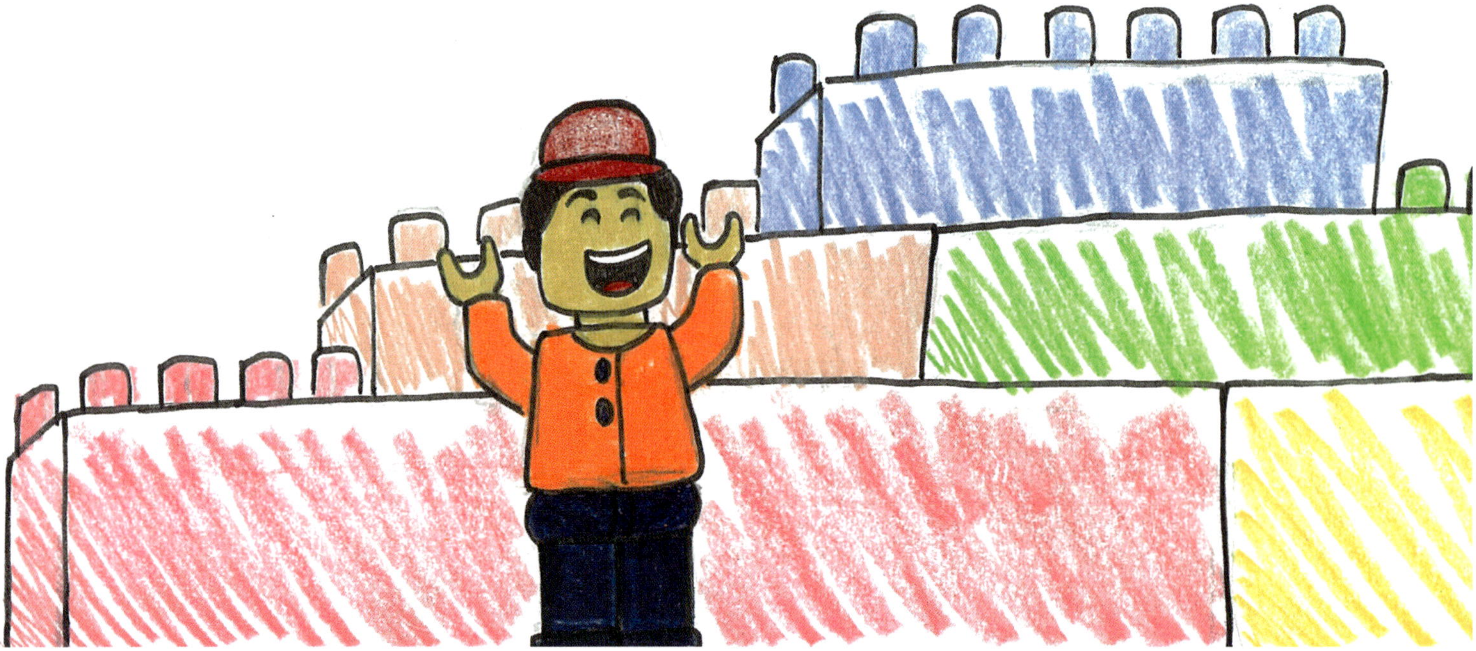

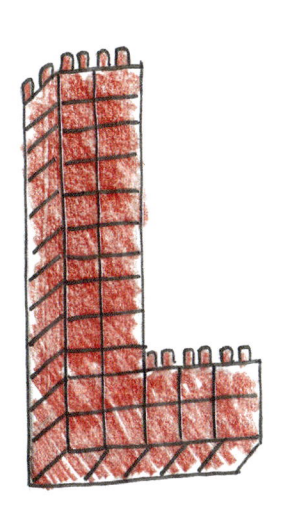

I love you more than...
all the LEGOs in LEGOLAND.

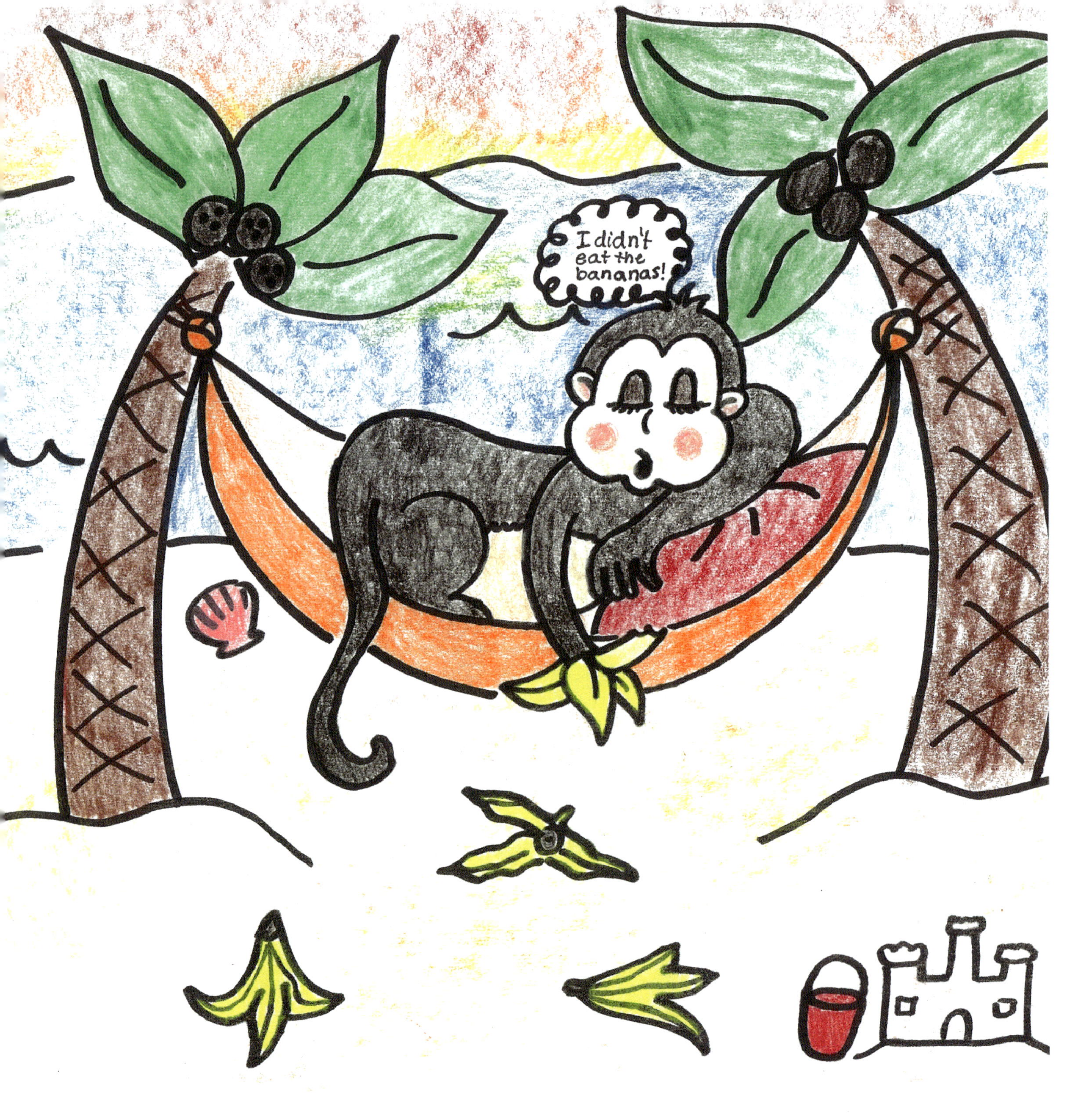
I didn't eat the bananas!

I love you more than...
all the bananas in the jungle.

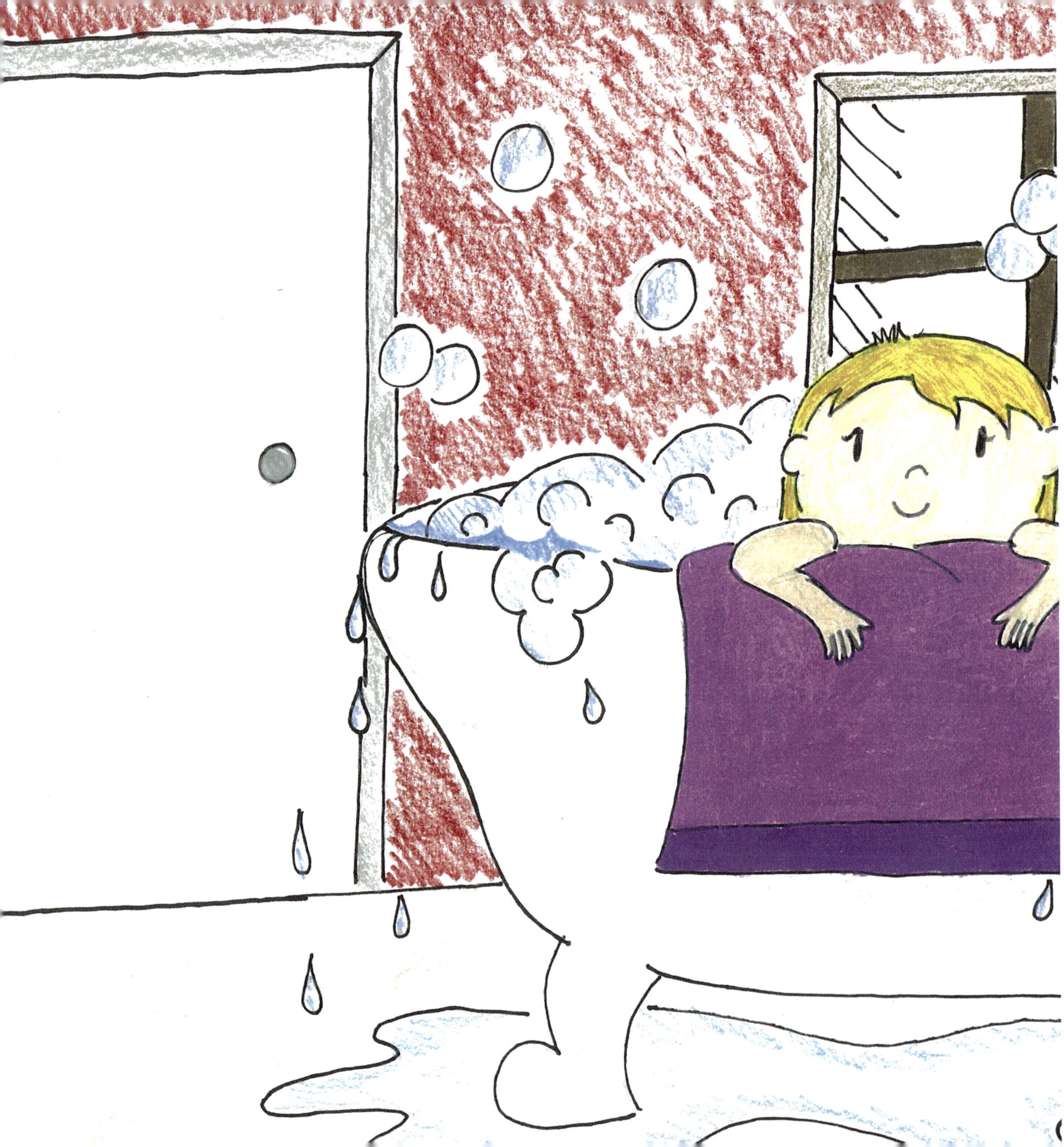

I love you more than...
all the bubbles in
my bubble bath.

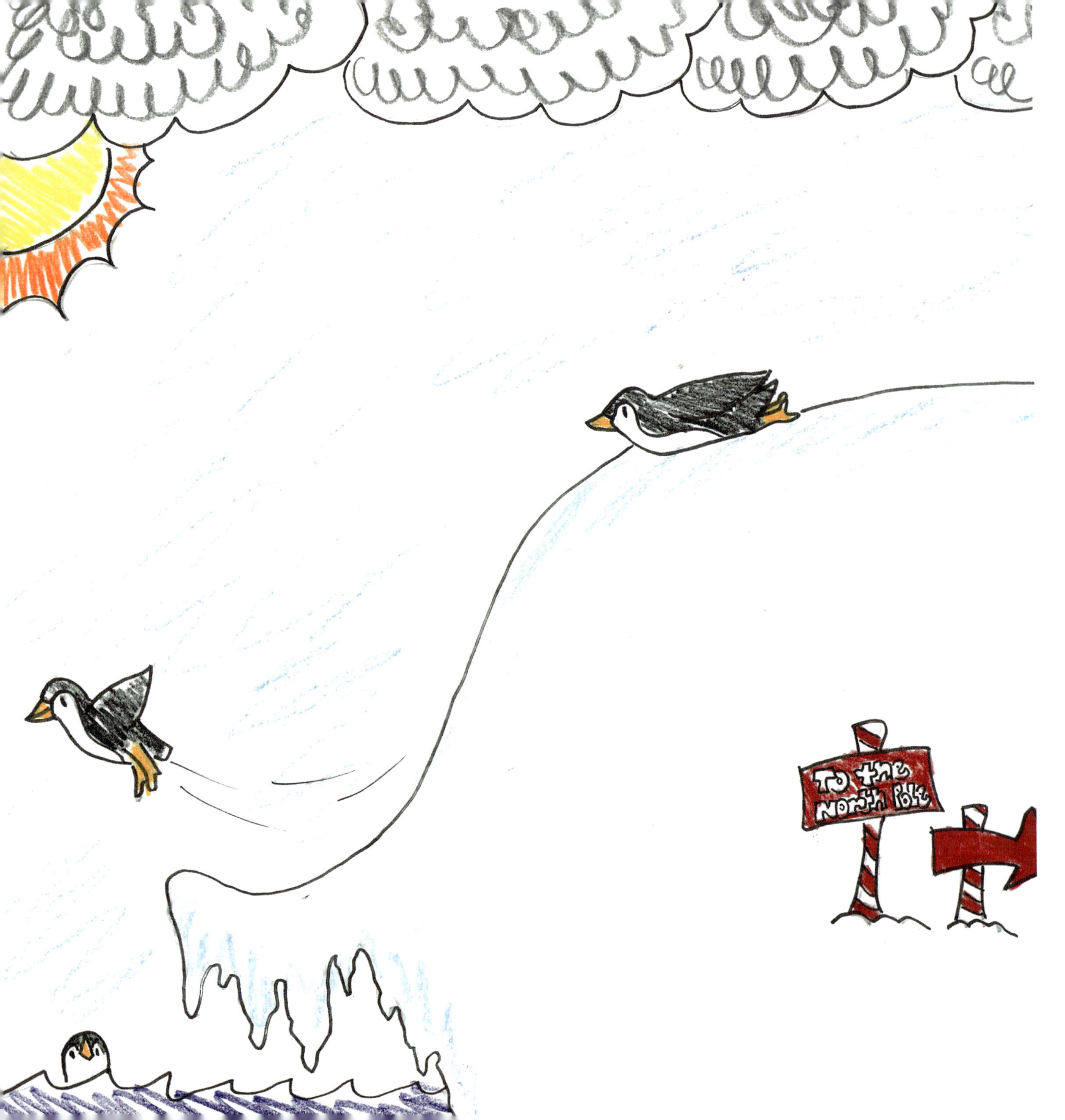
To the North Pole

I love you more than...
all the penguins in Antarctica.

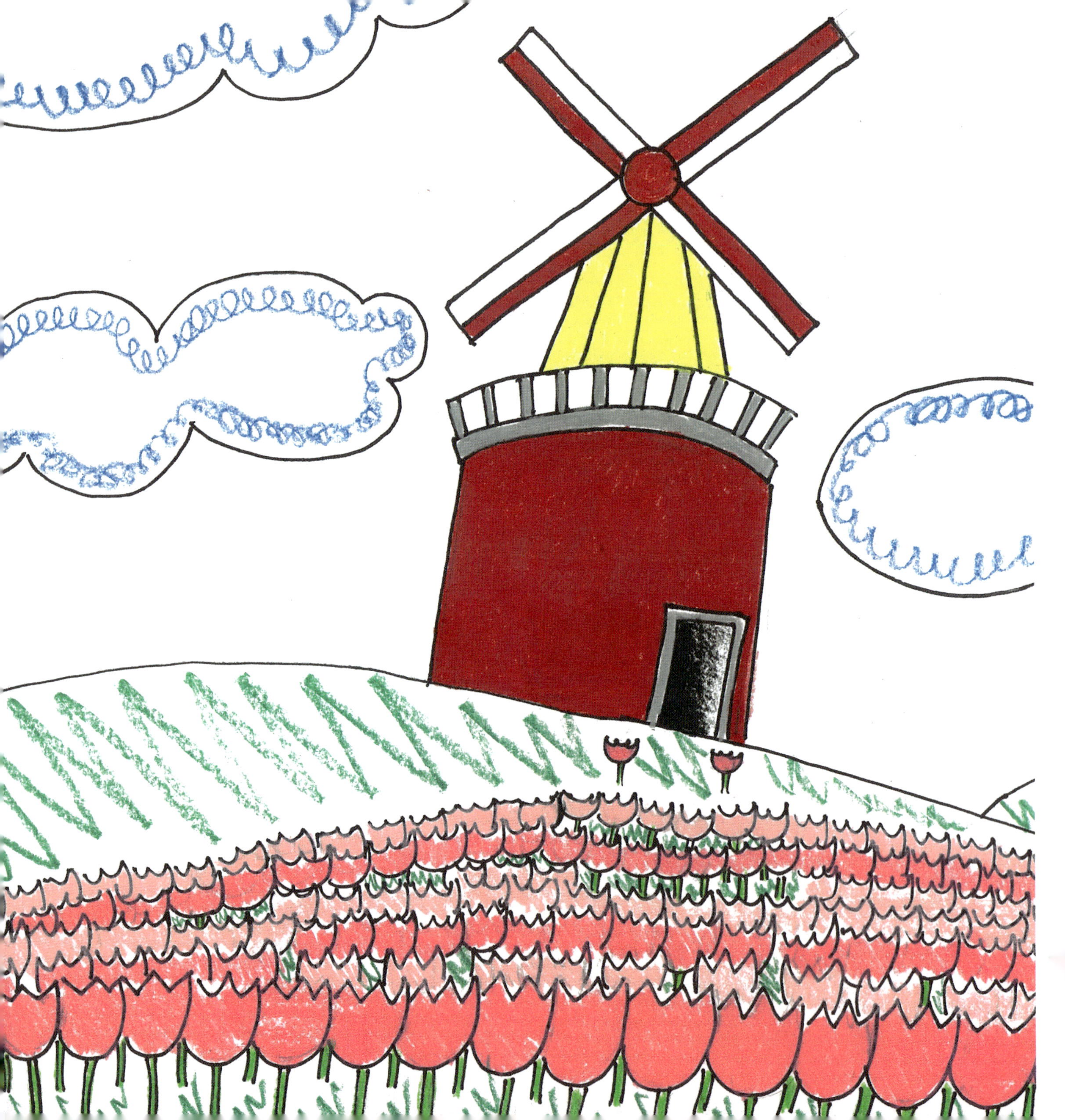

I love you more than...
all the tulips in Holland.

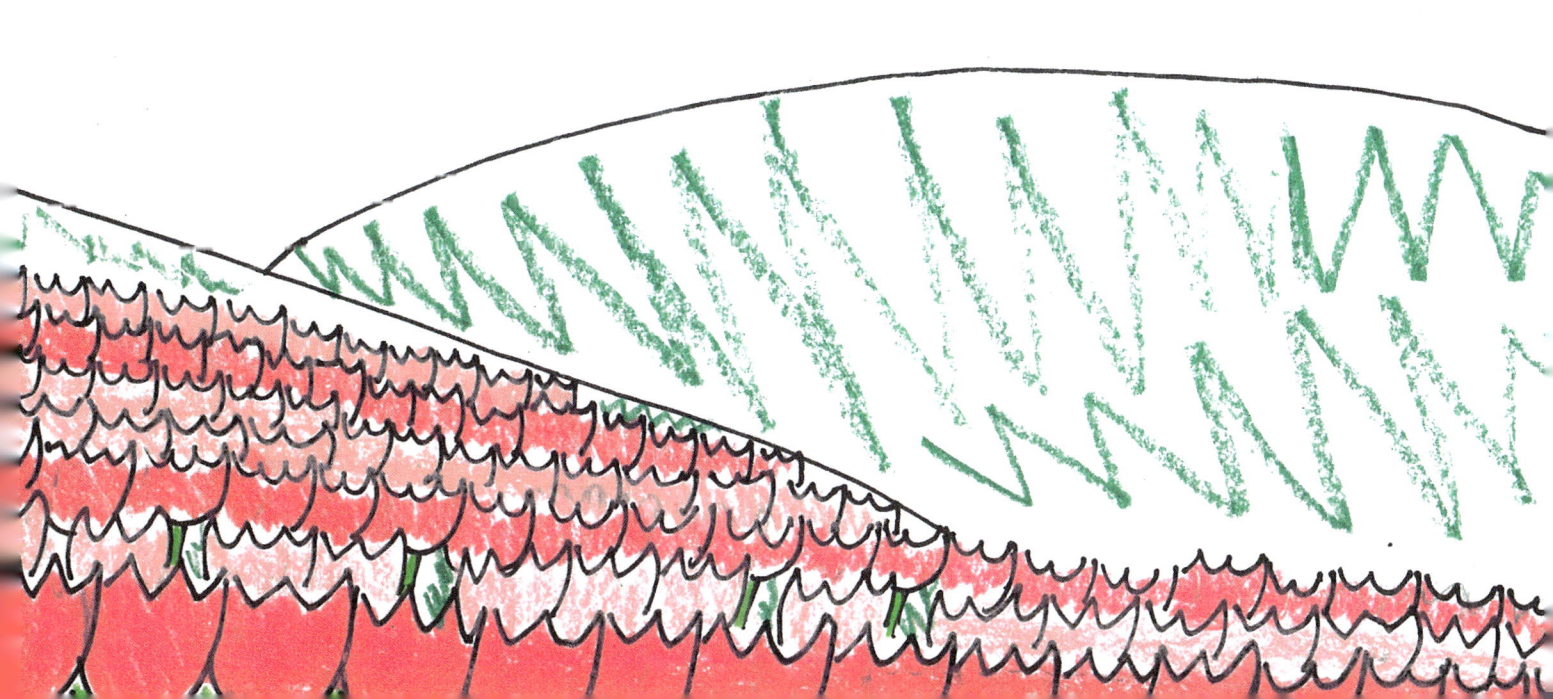

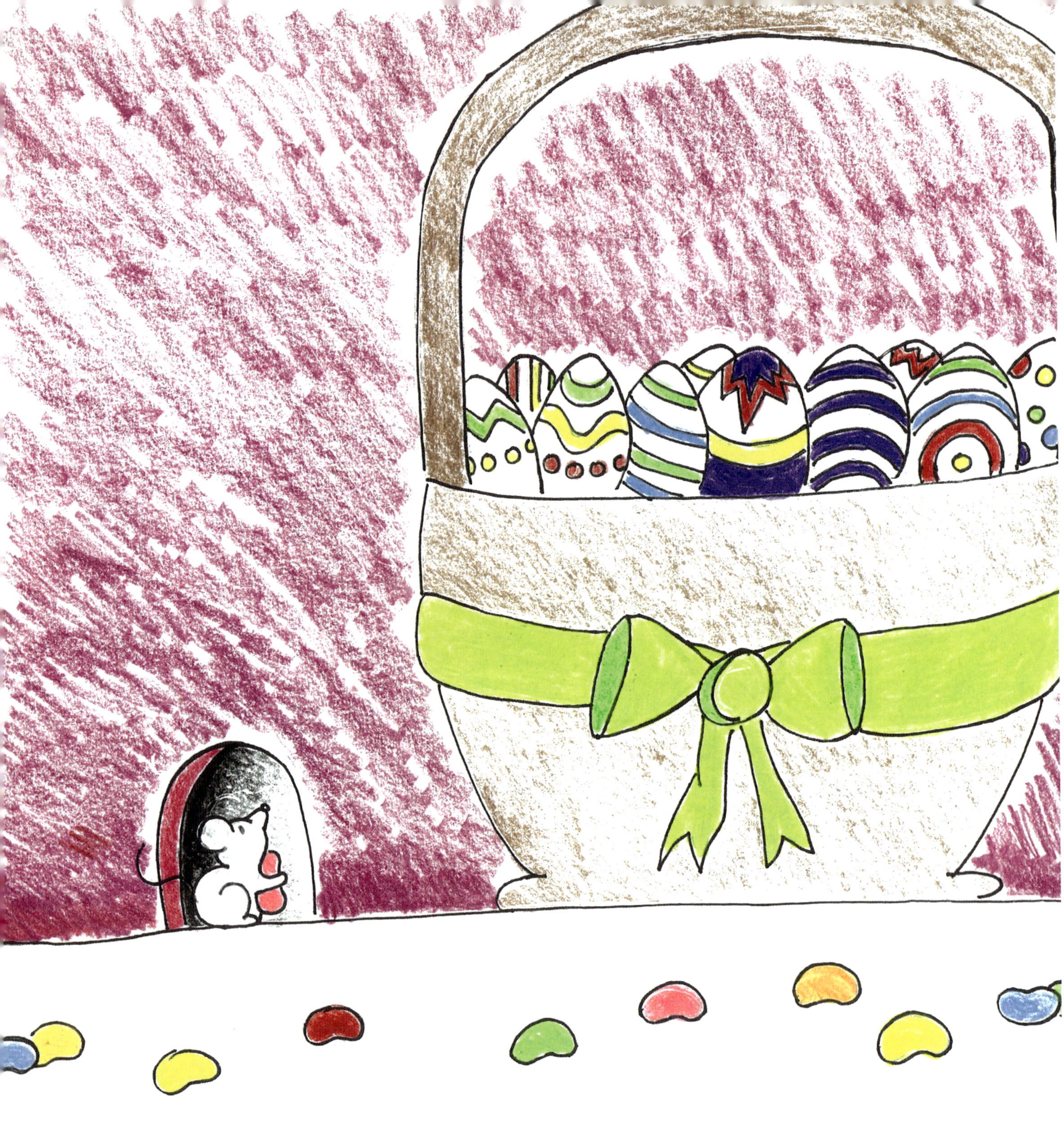

I love you more than...
all the jelly beans in the
Easter bunny's candy factory.

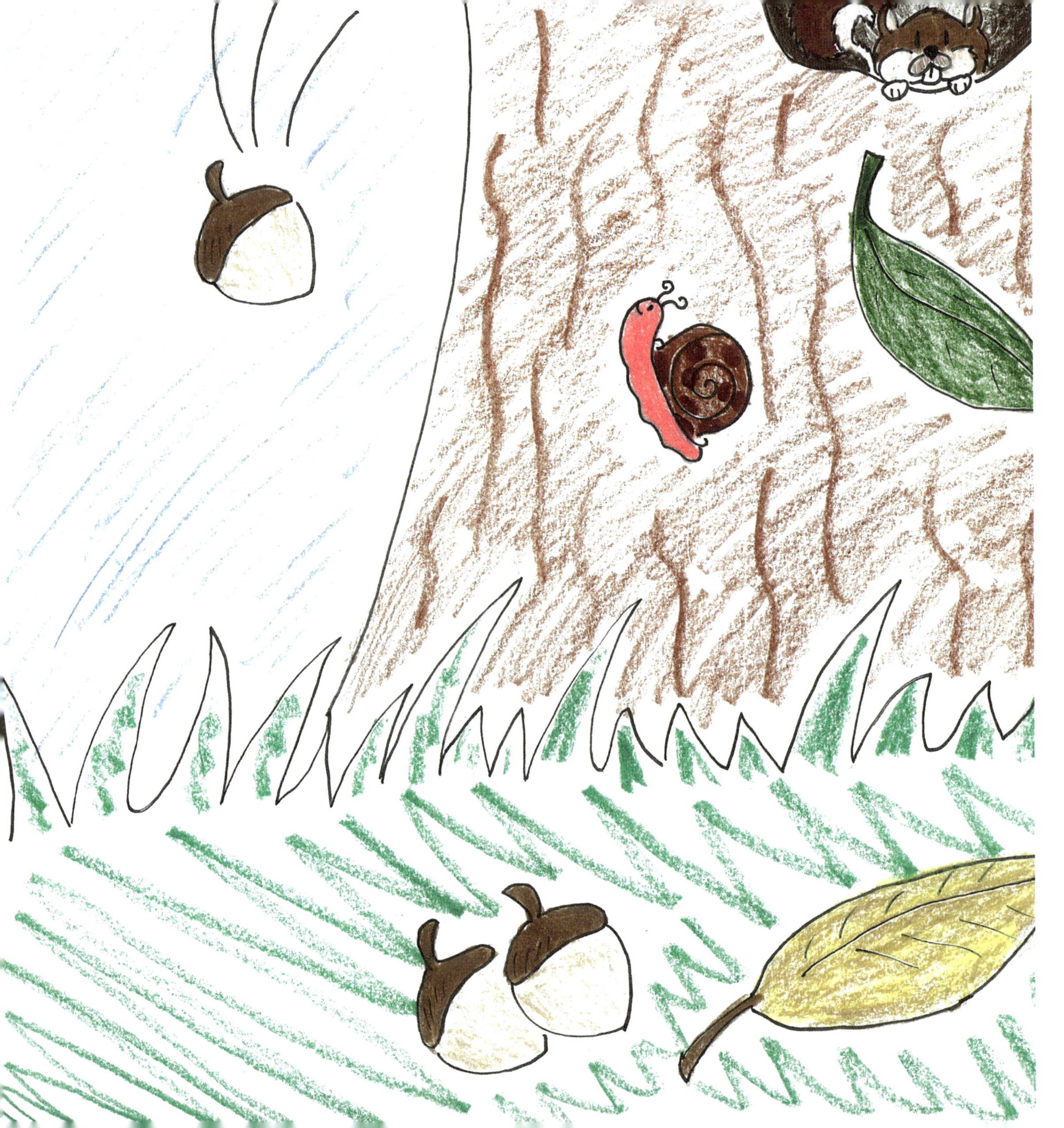

I love you more than...
all the acorns in the forest.

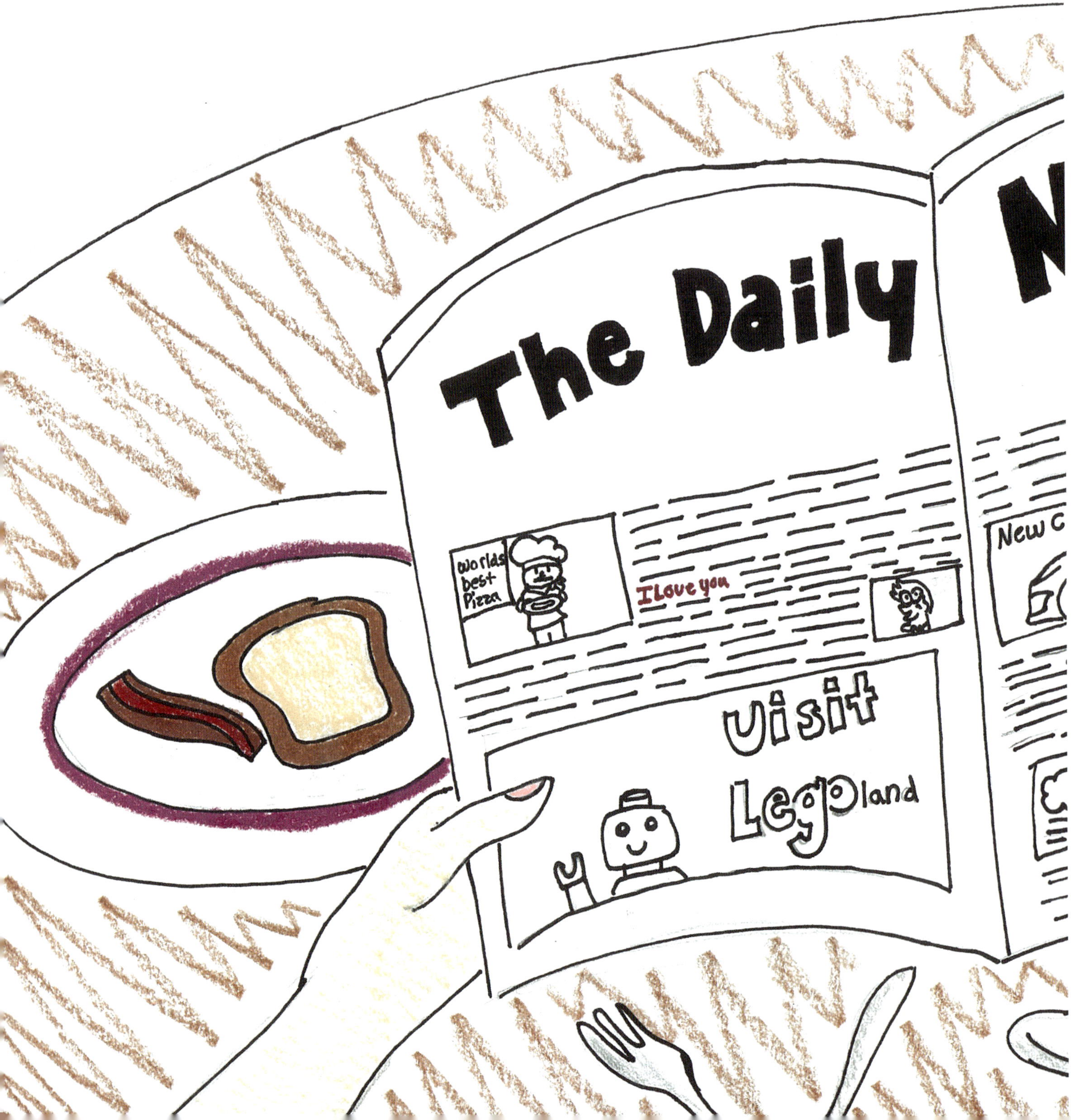
The Daily
Worlds best Pizza
I Love you
New C
Visit
Legoland

I love you more than...
all the words in the newspaper.

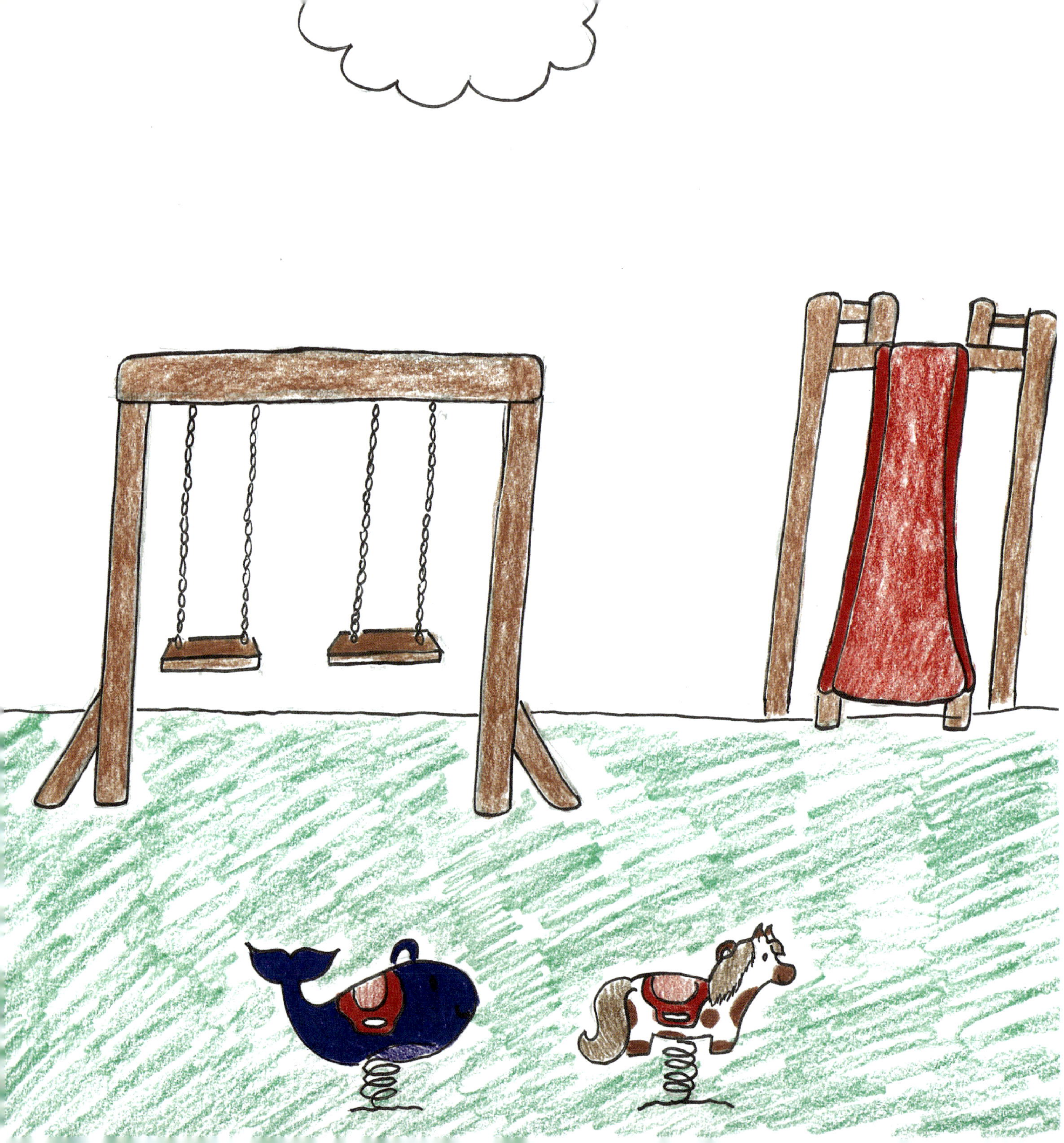

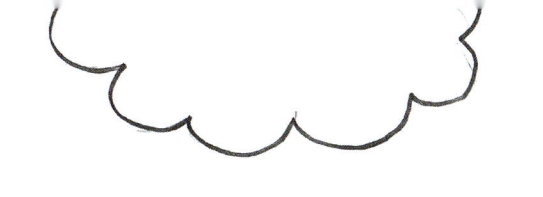

Now it's your turn!
Complete the sentence,
and draw your own picture.

I love you more than...

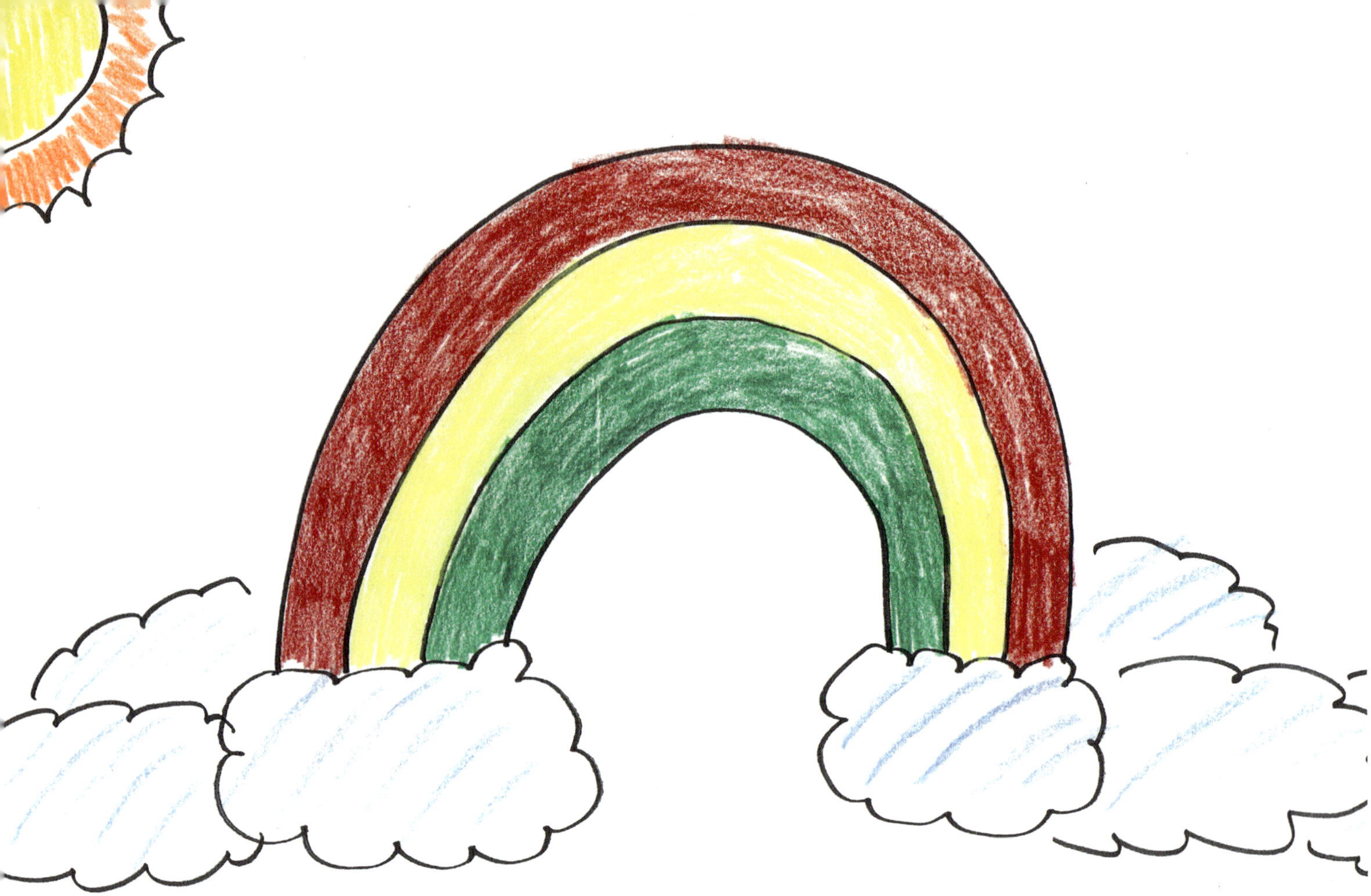

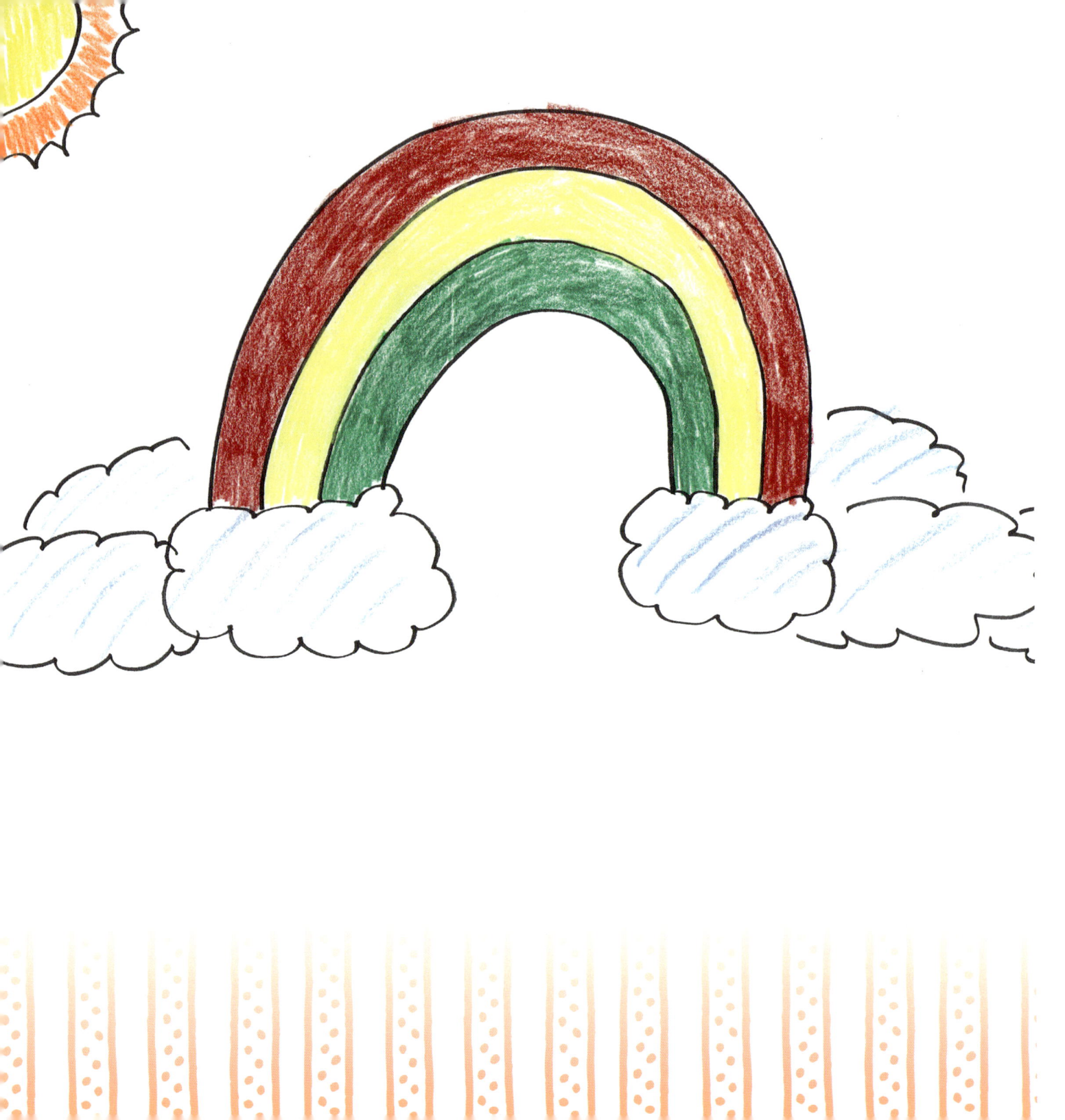

I love you more than...

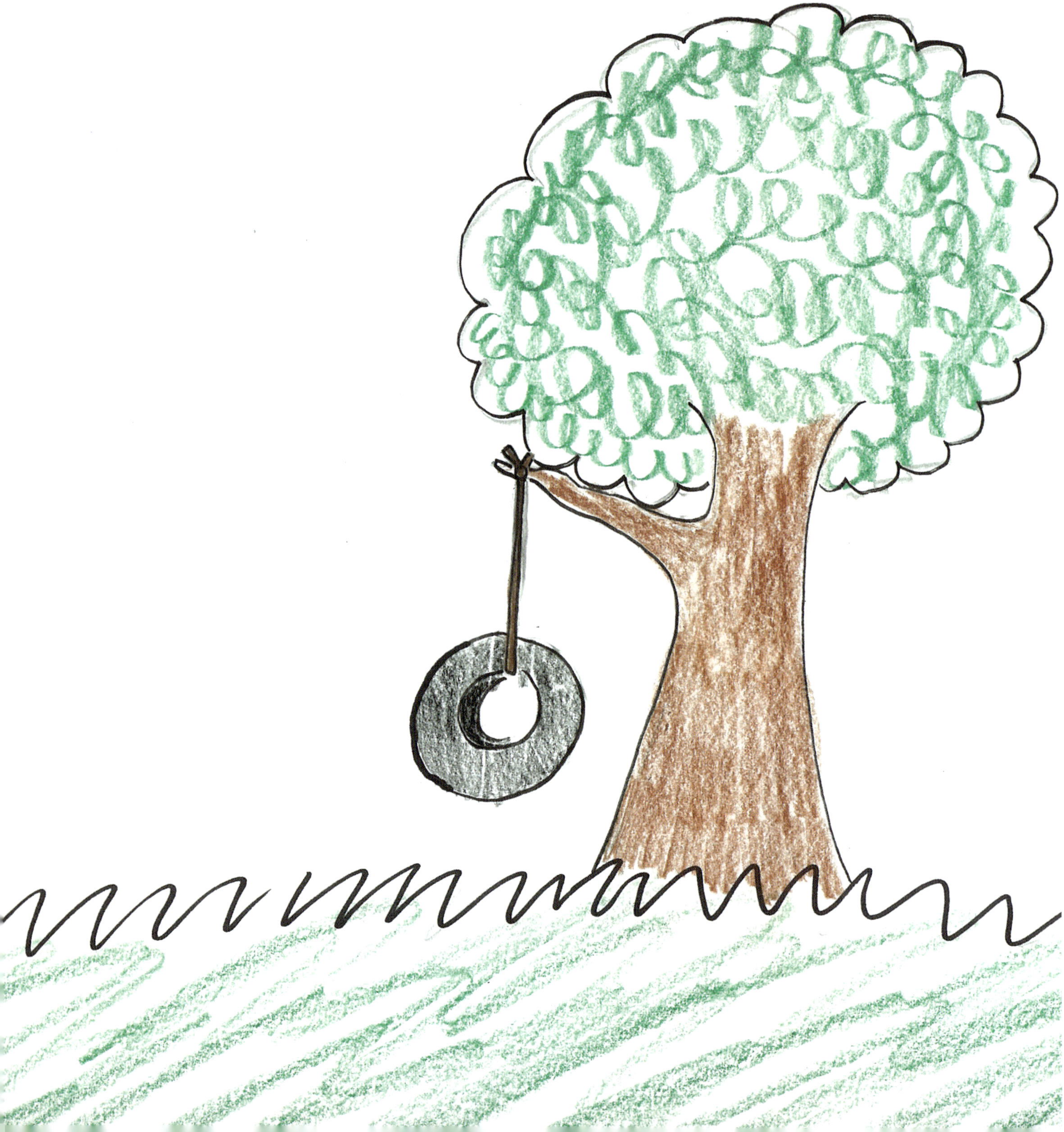

I love you more than...

I Love You More Than...

I love you more than...